THIRD-GRADE DETECTIVES #6

The Secret of the Green Skin

by
George E. Stanley
illustrated by
Salvatore Murdocca

ALADDIN PAPERBACKS

NEW YORK   LONDON   TORONTO   SYDNEY   SINGAPORE

*To Vivian Meshew—the best
mother-in-law in the world.*

This book is a work of fiction. Any references to historical events,
real people, or real locales are used fictitiously. Other names,
characters, places, and incidents are the product of the author's
imagination, and any resemblance to actual events or
locales or persons, living or dead, is entirely coincidental.

First Aladdin Paperbacks edition July 2003

Text copyright © 2003 by George Edward Stanley
Illustrations copyright © 2003 by Salvatore Murdocca

ALADDIN PAPERBACKS
An imprint of Simon & Schuster Children's Publishing Division
1230 Avenue of the Americas, New York, NY 10020

Also available in an Aladdin library edition.
Designed by Lisa Vega
The text of this book was set in 12-point Lino Letter.
Manufactured in the United States of America
8 10 9 7

Library of Congress Control Number for the library edition is
2002112082
ISBN-13: 978-0-689-85378-4
ISBN-10: 0-689-85378-5

Chapter One

Todd Sloan and Noelle Trocoderro hurried down the hall to Mr. Merlin's classroom.

They had been helping their principal, Mrs. Jenkins, put cans of food in a box for a family whose house had burned down.

Mrs. Jenkins told them they didn't need tardy slips.

She said she would call Mr. Merlin over the public-address system to tell him they were on their way.

That made Todd feel important.

Just then JoAnn Dickens passed them in the hall.

She didn't say anything.

That's strange, Todd thought. JoAnn was always friendly. He wondered what was wrong.

JoAnn was the new girl in their class.

Her family had been in town for only a couple of months.

They owned a family-style restaurant.

Todd and his parents were planning to eat there tonight.

"JoAnn!" Todd called. "Wait up!"

JoAnn stopped. She had tears in her eyes, and her nose was running.

"What's wrong?" Todd asked.

"Something terrible happened last night," JoAnn answered, sobbing.

"Some people who ate at our restaurant said my parents' cooking made them sick.

"They want the Health Department to shut us down.

"If that happens, we may have to move.

"I don't want to move. I like it here."

"How did the people get sick?" Noelle asked.

"It's a mystery," JoAnn said.

"We buy all of our food locally so that we know it's fresh, and we keep our kitchen spotless."

JoAnn let out another sob. "I don't want to talk about it. It makes me too sad."

She turned and hurried on down the hall.

Todd and Noelle followed her.

They reached Mr. Merlin's class just as JoAnn handed him her tardy slip.

The rest of the students were copying spelling words off the chalkboard.

They weren't paying any attention to JoAnn. They didn't notice that she had been crying.

"Let's tell Mr. Merlin about JoAnn," Todd whispered to Noelle.

"That's a good idea," Noelle whispered back.

Mr. Merlin's class was known as the Third-Grade Detectives.

They helped the police solve crimes.

Sometimes they worked with Dr. Smiley.

She was Mr. Merlin's friend.

She was also a police scientist.

Dr. Smiley even had a police laboratory in the basement of her home.

She used it when she needed to work on a mystery after she got home.

Dr. Smiley let the Third-Grade Detectives use her laboratory when they were trying to solve a mystery, too.

"Mr. Merlin," Noelle whispered, "I think we have a new mystery to solve."

Todd told Mr. Merlin what had happened at JoAnn's family's restaurant. "If we can prove it wasn't her parents' fault, then maybe the Health Department won't shut them down."

"And JoAnn won't have to move," Noelle added.

"I wondered what was upsetting her," Mr. Merlin said. "Well, you'll need to talk to JoAnn first. Make sure she won't mind if we try to solve the mystery for her."

Todd and Noelle decided to talk to JoAnn at recess.

They took their seats and started copying their spelling words.

"Study these words carefully," Mr. Merlin told the class when everyone was finished.

"We'll have a test on them tomorrow.

"Now get out your science books," he said. "We're going to talk about edible tubers."

"Yuck!" Leon Dennis said. "I'd never eat *tubers*!"

"Me either," Misty Goforth said.

"We eat them all the time at our house," Amber Lee Johnson said.

Todd looked at Noelle and rolled his eyes. He'd always thought there was something weird about Amber Lee's family.

Mr. Merlin didn't say anything.

He just smiled.

He probably thinks Amber Lee's family is weird, too, Todd thought.

Mr. Merlin told the class to turn to page 25 in their books.

Todd saw a picture of a *potato*!

He had been eating tubers all his life, and he hadn't even known it.

Todd looked over at Amber Lee.

Maybe she wasn't so weird after all, he decided.

Mr. Merlin told them all about potatoes.

They were usually grown from the *eyes* of other potatoes.

The eyes were really buds that grew on the potato skin.

These buds produced sprouts.

"That's what happens to our potatoes if we don't use them right away!" Misty said. "They grow lots of sprouts!"

"Exactly," Mr. Merlin said.

"With proper sunshine, the leaves produce more food than the plant can use," Mr. Merlin continued.

"That's when the leaves send the extra food down to be stored in the root of the potato plant.

"Potatoes are really just thick roots that grow underground.

"As the potatoes get bigger, their skin gets tougher and tougher.

"That keeps the moisture inside and protects the potato from bacteria that can cause it to rot.

"Potatoes are good for us.

"They're full of nutrients."

"I love all kinds of potatoes," Leon said. "Baked, fried, boiled, raw—"

Before Leon could finish, the recess bell rang, and Mr. Merlin's class headed outside.

JoAnn ran to a tree at the edge of the playground and sat down underneath it.

Todd and Noelle joined her.

They told JoAnn all about Mr. Merlin's Third-Grade Detectives.

"Now we want to solve your mystery," Todd said.

"Oh, that would be wonderful!" JoAnn said.

"Good!" Todd said. "When recess is over, we'll tell Mr. Merlin that the Third-Grade Detectives have a new case."

Chapter Two

When they got back to class, Todd told Mr. Merlin that JoAnn wanted them to solve her mystery.

"Good! I was hoping she would," Mr. Merlin said. "First, we'll let JoAnn tell us her story."

JoAnn was nervous, but Noelle agreed to stand beside her at the front of the room.

JoAnn gave Noelle a smile, took a deep breath, and told the class what happened at the restaurant.

"Now these people want to shut us down.

"They told the Health Department that we're not clean."

"You are clean!" Noelle protested. "The tablecloths don't have any spots on them!"

"That's not what the Health Department looks

for, Noelle," Amber Lee said. "They want to know if there are any bugs in the kitchen."

The class gasped.

"I found a bug in our kitchen once," Leon said. "I put it in a box and kept it."

"Class! Class! We're getting off the subject," Mr. Merlin said. He turned to JoAnn. "Tell us more about the food that you serve at your restaurant," he said.

"We buy our milk, cheese, and butter from Mr. Johnson's dairy farm," JoAnn said.

"That could be the problem, JoAnn! The milk might be bad!" Amber Lee said. "I drank some milk that was out of date one time, and I got really sick to my stomach."

The class nodded their agreement.

"What else?" Leon asked.

"We buy all our chickens and eggs from Mrs. Smith's poultry farm," JoAnn said.

"That's it! That's it!" Misty shouted. "I got really sick one time from eating a rotten egg!"

"Uuuugh!" the class groaned.

"Where do you get your vegetables?" Todd asked.

"From Mrs. Ruston's vegetable farm," JoAnn replied.

"Last week my brother and I even dug up some potatoes so my dad could make his famous potato skin soup."

"Oh, yuck!" Misty said. "That sounds awful!"

"It's not, though. It's delicious," Amber Lee said. "I ate some when the restaurant first opened."

"Everybody really likes it," JoAnn said.

"Is it hard to dig up potatoes?" Leon asked.

"Not really," JoAnn said.

"But it had rained, and the ground was muddy.

"So when we got back to the restaurant, we washed off the potatoes, then we put them in a sunny spot by a window so they would dry.

"My father used them to make his soup.

"And last night a lot of people got sick."

JoAnn sat down.

"I think it was the milk!" Amber Lee said.

Several people agreed with her.

"I think it was the eggs," Misty said.

Several people agreed with her.

"I think it was the bugs," Leon said.

"What bugs?" Noelle demanded. "I've never

seen any bugs in JoAnn's restaurant!"

"You can't always see bugs," Leon said.

"When I'm sick, my mother says I have a bug, but I've never seen one."

"Leon is talking about germs and bacteria," Mr. Merlin told them. "You can't see them, but they can really make you sick."

This was going to be a hard mystery, Todd decided. He could see milk and cheese and butter. He could see chickens and eggs. He could see potatoes. But if he couldn't see germs or bacteria, how would he know they were there?

Todd had an idea. "Give us a secret-code clue, Mr. Merlin," he said.

Mr. Merlin used to be a spy.

He gave the class secret-code clues to help them solve their mysteries.

Mr. Merlin said that solving secret codes also made their brains work better.

Todd wanted to make sure his brain always worked well.

"Okay," Mr. Merlin said.

He turned and started writing on the chalkboard.

13

He wrote:

2 2 - 4 2 - 1 5 - 1 5 - 3 3 - 2 4 - 4 3 - 1 4 -
1 1 - 3 3 - 2 2 - 1 5 - 4 2 - 3 4 - 4 5 - 4 3

Todd copied the secret-code clue onto a sheet of paper.

If Mr. Merlin's Third-Grade Detectives could solve it, maybe they could save JoAnn's family's restaurant.

Chapter Three

When the recess bell rang, Todd and Noelle raced for the new swing set at the edge of the playground.

"Numbers!" Todd shouted. "That means the secret-code clue has something to do with the alphabet!"

He was pumping as fast as he could.

He could see the roofs of the houses across the street from the school.

"That's what I thought at first, too, Todd," Noelle shouted, "but the numbers are too big.

"The first one is twenty-two, but the second one is forty-two!

"There are only twenty-six letters in the alphabet."

Todd thought about that for a minute.

"Number codes always have something to do with the alphabet, Noelle," he insisted. "We'll just have to figure out what it is."

For the next several minutes Todd and Noelle thought about the secret-code clue while they pretended they were in an airplane.

They flew over the ocean.

They flew over the mountains.

They went so high they almost flew over the top of the swing set.

Finally the bell rang.

When they got back to their class, Mr. Merlin said, "Did anyone solve the secret-code clue?"

No one had.

But Todd wasn't worried yet.

He was sure he'd be able to find a way to solve this one.

When he did, that would help them solve the mystery.

Mr. Merlin often let them work on a mystery in class, but today they were too busy.

First, they went to the gym for a test to see if their spines were straight.

Todd's was.

Then they went outside to hear people talk about the new sign in front of the school.

Todd's design had won third place.

A fifth grader beat him.

The fifth grader got a pizza party for his class.

Todd hoped they'd have another sign contest soon.

He wanted to win a pizza party for Mr. Merlin's class.

For the rest of the day they did math and writing.

When the bell rang to dismiss school, Todd said to Noelle, "Let's go to my house.

"My grandmother was going to bake a chocolate cake today.

"We can eat cake and try to solve the secret-code clue."

"Yes!" Noelle said.

She loved Todd's grandmother's chocolate cakes.

They tasted like fudge.

When they got to Todd's house, his grandmother was just finishing frosting the cake.

Todd thought his whole house smelled wonderful.

He and Noelle sat at the kitchen table.

While they ate cake, Todd wrote out the alphabet several ways.

He and Noelle tried to think of how the numbers in the clue would fit.

But nothing made sense.

Even two pieces of cake each couldn't help them solve it.

Just as Noelle was about to leave to go home, the doorbell rang.

Todd answered the door.

Amber Lee, Leon, and Misty were standing on the front porch.

"Have you solved the secret-code clue yet?" Amber Lee asked.

Todd and Noelle shook their heads.

"We haven't, either," Leon said, "but we do have some new information."

"What?" Noelle asked.

"Amber Lee didn't want us to tell you," Misty said, "but Mr. Merlin likes us to work together, so Leon and I outvoted her."

Amber Lee gave them dirty looks.

"My cousin works in the lab at the hospital," Misty said. "We told her that the people who complained to the Health Department accused JoAnn's parents of doing something wrong. She said if we can prove that some of the food was bad *before* it got to the restaurant, then it wouldn't be JoAnn's parents' fault."

"Yes!" Noelle said. "That's what we need to do!"

But where would they start to do that? Todd wondered.

They needed more help from Mr. Merlin.

Chapter Four

Todd could hear Noelle calling to him from the sidewalk in front of his house.

"Hurry, Mom! Noelle's already here!" Todd said. "I have to go! I don't want to be late for school."

"I'm almost finished," his mother said.

She was cutting the tags off his new shirt.

It had arrived yesterday afternoon in a birthday package from his uncle in New York.

The shirt was the latest style.

Todd had seen kids wearing shirts like this on television.

The kids at school would think he was so cool.

Finally his mother finished.

"It really needs to be pressed," she said.

"No, Mom!" Todd said. "It's supposed to look wrinkled!"

He hurriedly buttoned the shirt.

Then he grabbed his backpack and raced out the door.

"Hey! Cool shirt!" Noelle said. "I've seen those on television!"

Todd grinned. "My uncle sent it for my birthday."

Noelle gave him a funny look.

"Your birthday was two months ago," she said.

"I know," Todd said. "My uncle forgets."

"I wish people would forget my birthdays. That way I would get presents all year long," Noelle said. "Did you solve the secret-code clue?"

Todd shook his head. "I tried, but nothing worked," he said.

"We need a hint," Noelle said. "Maybe Mr. Merlin will give us a rule we can use."

Todd wished he could have solved the secret-code clue without a hint.

He was sure it had something to do with the alphabet, though.

Mr. Merlin had given them a number code before.

The numbers stood for the letters of the alphabet.

The number 1 stood for *A*.

The number 26 stood for *Z*.

Since some of these numbers went past 26, Todd had divided them.

But that still hadn't worked.

The second number in the code was 42.

When Todd divided that by 2, he got 21.

The twenty-first letter of the alphabet was *U*.

But that letter didn't make a word he recognized.

The first thing Mr. Merlin asked them was, "Has anyone solved the secret-code clue yet?"

No one had.

"Okay. I'll give you a rule," Mr. Merlin said. "Put the alphabet in a box, five squares by five squares."

"That won't work, Mr. Merlin," Amber Lee said.

"There are twenty-six letters in the alphabet!"

"There's one more part to the rule," Mr. Merlin said. "Two letters look alike, except that one is curved at the bottom. Put those together."

Now I know! Todd thought.

"I'll let you work on this for a while," Mr. Merlin said. "I know you all want to make sure JoAnn doesn't have to move."

Todd looked around the room.

He was sure several other kids knew what to do, too!

They all were writing fast.

Todd made a big square on a sheet of paper. He divided it into 25 smaller squares.

He put *1, 2, 3, 4,* and *5* at the top. He did the same thing along the left side.

In the top five squares he wrote *A, B, C, D,* and *E*. He finished writing the alphabet horizontally in the rest of the squares. In the square with *I,* he also wrote *J*. They looked alike—except *J* was curved at the bottom.

When he finished, his paper looked like this:

	1	2	3	4	5
1	A	B	C	D	E
2	F	G	H	I/J	K
3	L	M	N	O	P
4	Q	R	S	T	U
5	V	W	X	Y	Z

Quickly, Todd looked at the secret-code clue Mr. Merlin had given them: 2 2 - 4 2 - 1 5 - 1 5 - 3 3 - 2 4 - 4 3 - 1 4 - 1 1 - 3 3 - 2 2 - 1 5 - 4 2 - 3 4 - 4 5 - 4 3

He used the alphabet square to decode it:

GREEN IS DANGEROUS!

He raised his hand a split second before Amber Lee.

"Yes, Todd," Mr. Merlin said.

"Green is dangerous!" Todd said.

"You're right! So try to solve JoAnn's mystery

over the weekend," Mr. Merlin said. "Now it's time for art."

"This is going to be easy," Noelle whispered to Todd.

"How?" Todd asked.

"Think about it, Todd. What turns *green* on food that can make you sick?" Noelle said. "*Mold!* If we find some mold, we'll solve this mystery!"

Chapter Five

Todd and Noelle ran down the front steps of the school.

"I'm glad it's Friday," Noelle said.

"I am, too," Todd said. "We have all weekend to look for mold."

Amber Lee, Leon, and Misty were standing together on the sidewalk. They were talking to JoAnn.

"Come on, Noelle!" Todd said. "We need to find out what they're saying."

"We're going to JoAnn's restaurant tomorrow morning to look for clues," Misty told them.

"The restaurant is closed for a few days, so there won't be anybody there," JoAnn told them sadly.

"We know what to look for," Todd said.

"What?" Amber Lee said.

"Mold!" Noelle said.

JoAnn's eyes got big. "We don't have any mold in our restaurant."

"We've got lots of mold at our house," Leon said. "The refrigerator is full of it!"

"Yuck, Leon!" Amber Lee said. "You shouldn't tell people things like that."

"Sorry, Leon," Noelle said. "Your mold won't help us solve JoAnn's mystery."

"Hey! Maybe it's mold *in the air*. I've heard my dad complain about that before," Todd said. "He'll sneeze, and then he'll say, 'It's all this mold in the air.'"

"We don't even have mold in the air in our restaurant," JoAnn insisted. "My parents won't allow it!"

"There's probably mold everywhere, JoAnn," Amber Lee said. "That doesn't mean your restaurant isn't clean."

"Well, if we can't *see* any mold on the food from the restaurant, we can still take samples and look at it under Dr. Smiley's microscopes," Todd said.

"If we find mold then, we can tell if it was in the food before it got to JoAnn's family's restaurant," Noelle said. "That would mean it's not her parents' fault."

"How can you tell that?" Misty asked.

Amber Lee was waving her hand. "I know! I know! We studied that in science!" she said.

Noelle rolled her eyes. "Amber Lee, we're not in school now. You don't have to ask permission to talk."

"Mold grows in stages, just like plants," Amber Lee said excitedly. "Dr. Smiley can tell us how long the mold has been growing!"

"Remember that piece of bread we used for an experiment?" Noelle said. "Mr. Merlin told us that mold was growing in it even before we could see it."

"Oh, yeah! It got greener and greener," Leon said. "I really thought it was beautiful."

"We'll find out when the food was delivered," Todd said. "If the mold was growing on it before then, JoAnn's parents are in the clear!"

Everyone agreed that looking for mold was a great idea.

So they decided to meet at JoAnn's restaurant the next morning to collect food samples.

The next morning Todd and Noelle rode their bicycles to JoAnn's restaurant.

Amber Lee, Misty, and Leon were waiting outside.

Soon JoAnn and her brother, Phil, arrived on their bicycles.

Phil was in the sixth grade.

He played football.

Todd thought he was really good.

"Phil's going to clean up the restaurant," JoAnn said. "He said we could look for evidence while he did that."

"I hope you find something. I don't want to move, either," Phil said. "I'm supposed to be the quarterback next year. The team needs me."

While Phil cleaned the restaurant, the Third-Grade Detectives looked around the kitchen.

They didn't find green mold on anything in the cabinets or in the refrigerator.

"I told you so," JoAnn said.

"Well, we still need to collect food samples," Todd said.

He and Noelle got some milk, some cheese, and some butter.

Amber Lee, Leon, and Misty got some chicken and some eggs.

"What about the vegetables?" Misty asked.

The Third-Grade Detectives thought for a minute.

Finally Amber said, "Whoever heard of vegetables making you sick?"

"Yeah!" Leon said. "My parents are always telling me to eat my vegetables so I'll be healthy."

"Okay, then. Let's take our evidence to Dr. Smiley," Todd said. "She's expecting us."

They rode their bicycles over to Dr. Smiley's house.

She had her laboratory already set up.

Dr. Smiley made slides of all the evidence.

The Third-Grade Detectives looked into the microscopes.

They saw all kinds of funny-looking things.

But Dr. Smiley told them that she saw no mold.

Todd had a sudden thought.

"What about *bacteria*?" he asked. "Do you see any green bacteria?"

"Good thinking, Todd," Dr. Smiley said. "I do see green bacteria, but they're all *good* bacteria."

Todd was disappointed.

"What do we do now?" he asked. "If it's not mold or *bad* bacteria, then what else is green that can make people sick?"

"I think you need to ask Mr. Merlin for another secret-code clue," Dr. Smiley said.

Chapter Six

Monday morning Mr. Merlin's class talked about the green stuff they had found.

A few of the Third-Grade Detectives had gone to Mrs. Smith's poultry farm.

"We found some green bugs," they reported. "The chickens were eating them."

Todd looked at Mr. Merlin.

Did that mean the mystery had been solved?

"It's normal for chickens to eat bugs," he replied. "All colors. That wouldn't make people sick."

Some of the other Third-Grade Detectives had gone to Mr. Johnson's dairy farm.

"Some of the hay looked green," they reported. "The cows were eating it."

"That's normal, too," Mr. Merlin said. "That's what cows eat."

Todd told the class about the trip to JoAnn's restaurant.

"We looked everywhere," he said, "but we didn't find any green mold.

"Next, we took samples of the food to Dr. Smiley's laboratory.

"We didn't see any mold under the microscope, and all the *green* bacteria were good."

"Great job, Third-Grade Detectives!" Mr. Merlin said.

"Solving mysteries isn't easy.

"But you're all on the right track."

Todd wasn't sure they were. But if Mr. Merlin thought they were, then maybe he shouldn't feel so bad.

"Dr. Smiley said we needed another secret-code clue," Noelle said.

"Okay," Mr. Merlin said.

He turned and started writing on the chalkboard.

He wrote:

54 - 23 - 11 - 33 - 52 - 32 - 41 - 25 -
22 - 33 - 12 - 22 - 42 - 32 - 33 - 31 -
32 - 42 - 15 - 42 - 32 - 11 - 43

The class got excited.

They started trying to decode the new secret message.

They were using the code that Mr. Merlin had given them the other day.

But Todd was sure that wouldn't work.

Mr. Merlin never gave them the same secret-code twice.

He always made changes.

Todd tested the first few letters to make sure he was right.

54 - 22 - 11 - 33 - 52 - 32 was Y - G - A - N - W - M. *Yganwm*.

He was.

Yganwm wasn't any English word he had ever seen!

Mr. Merlin let them work on the new secret-code clue for several minutes.

By the time the recess bell rang, no one had figured it out.

JoAnn looked as if she was going to cry again.

She probably thinks the Third-Grade Detectives aren't very good at solving mysteries, Todd thought.

"Come on, Todd! We're going to play kickball," Leon said. "It's us against the other third-grade class."

"Not now. I have to solve this secret code," Todd said. "It's important to JoAnn."

Leon whispered something to Amber Lee and Misty.

They told the rest of the class.

"We won't play kickball, either," Leon announced. "We'd rather help JoAnn, too."

Mr. Merlin's Third-Grade Detectives all grabbed pencils and paper.

Then they went outside and sat down under a tree.

"I think this is a variation of the first code Mr. Merlin gave us," Todd explained to them.

"That's what he usually does."

"So we need to move the numbers and the

letters around until something makes sense?" Noelle said.

"Right," Todd told them.

The Third-Grade Detectives started writing.

They tried all kinds of variations.

Finally Todd said, "I think I've got it.

"It's not that hard!

"You leave the numbers where they are, but you switch the letters around."

He showed the Third-Grade Detectives what he meant.

He divided a square into 25 smaller squares.

He wrote 1, 2, 3, 4, and 5 across the top squares.

He did the same along the left-hand side.

"But this time I'll start the alphabet on the right-hand side," Todd explained.

He wrote A under 5 and continued across the top.

On the second row he wrote F under 5 and continued until he had filled in all the blanks.

He put I and J together again.

"Now, let's see if we can solve this second secret-code clue," Todd said.

	1	2	3	4	5
1	E	D	C	B	A
2	K	J/I	H	G	F
3	P	O	N	M	L
4	U	T	S	R	Q
5	Z	Y	X	W	V

Using the new secret code, the Third-Grade Detectives started to decode the message.

They all finished at the same time.

"Something's still wrong," Amber Lee said. "I don't understand this message."

Todd was glad that he had figured out the new secret code without getting a rule from Mr. Merlin.

But he didn't understand it, either.

He could read the words, but they didn't make any sense:

. . . *when you find it on potatoes!*

Chapter Seven

Green is dangerous . . . when you find it on potatoes, Todd thought.

Was Mr. Merlin talking about *mold*? Todd wondered.

He had begun to think that wasn't what they should be looking for.

JoAnn was right, he decided. Her parents would have noticed if their potatoes—as well as the other food—had been green and moldy!

The Third-Grade Detectives must be on the wrong track.

Sometimes that happened to *police* detectives, he knew.

Dr. Smiley had told them so.

"This is hard," Amber Lee said. "We'll never solve the mystery now."

"Yes, we will!" Todd assured her. "Mr. Merlin's Third-Grade Detectives never give up!"

The recess bell rang.

Everyone hurried back to Mr. Merlin's classroom.

Todd told him that they had solved the secret-code clue.

Amber Lee added, "And it doesn't make any sense! Potatoes are brown on the outside and white on the inside."

The rest of the class agreed.

"Well, that means you still have some detective work to do," Mr. Merlin told them.

Several kids asked him for another rule, but Mr. Merlin said they had all the rules they needed.

"Mr. Merlin is getting tough," Noelle whispered to Todd.

Todd nodded, but he wasn't sure he really believed that.

Maybe Mr. Merlin just wanted them to *think* harder about the mystery.

He was always telling them that people didn't *think* enough today.

What were they missing? Todd wondered.

For the rest of the day, it was hard for Todd to keep his mind on what they were doing in class.

But just as the final bell rang, Todd suddenly had a great idea.

"We need to go to Mrs. Ruston's vegetable farm and dig up some potatoes," he whispered to Noelle.

"We need to look for *green*."

"I agree with Amber Lee, Todd," Noelle said. "Potatoes are brown on the outside and white on the inside."

"That's what everybody thinks, Noelle," Todd said.

"But we must be missing something.

"We have to follow Mr. Merlin's secret-code clue if we want to solve this mystery."

"Okay," Noelle said.

Todd went with Noelle to her house.

Noelle told her mother that she thought helping JoAnn and her family was more important than cleaning up her room.

Her mother let out a big sigh, but she said Noelle could go with Todd to Mrs. Ruston's vegetable farm because she wanted some fresh vegetables for dinner.

She gave Noelle a list and some money.

"Don't forget to get the vegetables after you dig up the potatoes," she told Noelle.

"I won't, Mom," Noelle said.

Todd and Noelle rode their bicycles to Mrs. Ruston's farm at the edge of town.

They told Mrs. Ruston they wanted to dig up some potatoes.

"People just love to do this," Mrs. Ruston said. "That way they know they're getting *fresh* potatoes."

She gave them a couple of hoes and told them where to dig.

As he and Noelle dug, Todd thought about what Mr. Merlin had told them about potatoes.

It was fascinating how they grew.

Finally Todd and Noelle had dug up enough potatoes to fill a small straw basket.

"This should be enough," Todd said.

"JoAnn was right about potatoes," Noelle said. "They sure are dirty."

"We'll take them to my house," Todd said. "We'll wash them off and see if we can find any green on them."

Noelle got the other vegetables her mother wanted.

She paid for those, and Todd paid for the potatoes.

When they got back to Todd's house, they took the potatoes to the backyard.

Todd got a garden hose and washed them off.

He and Noelle looked at them carefully.

"I don't see green anywhere," Noelle said.

"Me either," Todd said. "You and Amber Lee were right. Potatoes are brown on the outside and white on the inside."

Todd and Noelle went into Todd's house.

They left the potatoes on the patio table so the sun would dry them.

"I can't think of any other way to solve this mystery, Noelle," Todd said. "I guess we're not very good detectives after all."

Chapter Eight

The next morning at school Todd told the class that he and Noelle had gone to Mrs. Ruston's farm.

"We dug up some potatoes and took them to my house.

"We washed off the dirt and looked at them carefully.

"But we didn't see any green.

"So we left them out on the patio to dry."

"We don't know what else to do, Mr. Merlin," Noelle said. "We've failed. If JoAnn has to move, it'll be our fault."

JoAnn started crying.

Several girls put their arms around her shoulders.

"Don't give up," Mr. Merlin said. "You may be able to solve the mystery this afternoon."

Todd looked at Mr. Merlin.

"What do you mean?" he asked.

"You and JoAnn both did something that you should never do," Mr. Merlin said.

Everyone in the class looked at them.

"What did they do?" Misty asked.

"If I tell you, then it won't be the Third-Grade Detectives who solve the mystery," Mr. Merlin said.

"You need to figure this out for yourself.

"When good detectives are stumped, they always go back over all the steps they've taken.

"They re-examine everything carefully.

"That's what you all should do."

The Third-Grade Detectives wanted to think about that now, but Mr. Merlin said, "No. We have to practice our parts for the school program next week."

Todd definitely didn't want to do that.

He couldn't understand why all school plays were so silly.

For this play all the kids in Mr. Merlin's class were flowers.

Except for Todd and Noelle.

Noelle was a watering can.

49

Todd was the sun.

The class wore hats that looked like flowers.

They had green cloth tubes around their bodies.

These represented the stems.

The front side of the stem was light green.

The back side of the stem was dark green.

Everyone was supposed to stand in a long line across the stage with the light green part showing first.

On cue, Noelle came out onstage and pretended to water the flowers.

She was followed by Todd, the sun.

As Todd passed each flower, the person would slowly turn, so that the dark green side of the stem would be seen.

The point of this, Mr. Merlin said, was to show that with plenty of water and sunshine, plants turn green.

The class put on their costumes.

They followed Mr. Merlin to the auditorium.

One of the fourth-grade classes had agreed to be an audience for the rehearsal.

Todd could already hear the fourth graders giggling.

Why do we have to rehearse in front of people who make fun of us? Todd wondered.

The flowers lined up onstage.

The music teacher started playing the piano.

Noelle pranced out onstage.

She pretended to water the flowers.

The fourth graders giggled until their teacher told them to be quiet.

Now it was Todd's turn.

The sun came out onstage.

As he passed each flower, it turned green.

Just as Todd reached the middle flower, he stopped.

"Yes!" he cried. "I know what JoAnn, Noelle, and I did wrong!"

Chapter Nine

Todd was glad he was in Mr. Merlin's third-grade class.

He was sure that the other third-grade teacher would be really upset with him because he yelled during the middle of the play.

But not Mr. Merlin.

In fact, Mr. Merlin seemed almost as excited as Todd.

When the play was finally over, the Third-Grade Detectives hurriedly changed into their regular clothes.

"JoAnn and her family won't have to move after all," Todd announced to everyone.

The class cheered.

"We need to meet at Dr. Smiley's house after school," Todd said.

He looked at JoAnn. "Is there any of your father's potato skin soup left?" he asked.

JoAnn nodded. "I saw the container in the refrigerator when we were getting evidence the other day," she said.

"Bring it," Todd said.

He looked at Noelle.

"We'll bring our evidence, too," he said.

Noelle looked puzzled.

But she didn't say anything until after school, when they were on their way to Todd's house.

"What *evidence*?" Noelle asked.

"The potatoes we dug up at Mrs. Ruston's vegetable farm," Todd replied.

Noelle stopped. "Todd! We looked at those potatoes!" Noelle said. "They didn't have any green on them."

Todd grinned. "Not then they didn't," he said.

When they got to Todd's house, they went to the backyard.

The potatoes were still on the patio table.

The sun had dried them.

The potato skins were still brown.

But now they also had a light green cast to them.

Noelle gasped. "What happened?" she said.

"I'm not sure," Todd said, "but I bet Dr. Smiley can help us figure it out."

They put the potatoes in a basket and headed to Dr. Smiley's house.

Mr. Merlin and the rest of the Third-Grade Detectives were already in Dr. Smiley's laboratory.

JoAnn had brought the container of her father's potato skin soup.

Mr. Merlin asked Todd to tell them what he thought had made the people in the restaurant sick.

"Well, I don't really know what it is," Todd said, "but I think I know how it happened."

He grinned. "I thought the play was silly, but it gave me the answer," he said.

"When plants are exposed to sunlight, they turn green.

"JoAnn and her brother washed off the potatoes they dug up at Mrs. Ruston's vegetable farm.

"They left them in the sun to dry.

"Her father used those potatoes to make potato skin soup.

"The people in their restaurant got sick.

"We thought it was because of something else they ate.

"Noelle and I dug up some potatoes, too.

"When we washed them off, we didn't see any green.

"But we also left them in the sun to dry.

"And the next day we could see a light green cast under the skin.

"Mr. Merlin's secret-code clues said, *'Green is dangerous when you find it on potatoes.'*"

"Mr. Merlin is right," Dr. Smiley said.

"When potatoes are exposed to sunlight, the sunlight produces solanine.

"That's the green you see.

"It's poisonous, and it can make you very sick.

"When you see any green on potatoes, you should always remove it before you use the potatoes for a meal."

"Oh! What about those little green places that you sometimes see on potato chips?" Amber Lee said. "Will those make you sick?"

"No. The high temperature of deep frying cooks the solanine out of the potato chips," Dr. Smiley said, "but since JoAnn's father's soup wasn't cooked at such a high temperature, the solanine was still in it."

She took a sample of the potato skin soup and put it in a glass beaker.

She added some chemicals and shook it.

In a couple of minutes Dr. Smiley nodded.

"It tests positive for solanine," she said.

"Oh, no! This was all my fault!" JoAnn said. "Our restaurant will be closed, and we'll have to move."

"I don't think so," Dr. Smiley said.

"This is not something the Health Department would close a restaurant for.

"But you've all learned a very good lesson: Potatoes should always be stored in a dark, dry place.

"They should never be stored where they're exposed to sunlight."

Two days later Dr. Smiley, Mr. Merlin, and the Third-Grade Detectives met at JoAnn's family's restaurant.

There had been a big story in the newspaper.

It told how the Third-Grade Detectives had solved the mystery of what had made people sick.

The newspaper even published a letter of apology from JoAnn!

Todd noticed that the restaurant was full.

Now that people knew the real story about what had happened, they had come back there to eat.

"You saved our restaurant," JoAnn's father told them.

"You may order anything on the menu."

The Third-Grade Detectives looked at one another and grinned. They all wanted the same thing.

"We'll start with your famous potato skin soup!" Todd said with a grin.

Once the Third-Grade Detectives had solved a mystery, there was nothing to worry about!

WHO'S THE THIEF?

This experiment works best if it's conducted right after students have been walking around on the playground during recess. (It's important that the soles of their shoes be coated with dust.)

1. The teacher will choose six students for this experiment. One student will be the detective. The remaining five students will be suspects. It's important to make sure each suspect is wearing a different type or brand of shoe.

2. During recess these five students will choose among themselves who is going to be the thief. They won't tell anyone else who it is.

3. Before the rest of the class returns from

recess, the teacher and the detective will put a "valuable object" on a small table near the door of the classroom.

4. They will tape a piece of white butcher paper on the floor in front of the table so that the "thief" will have to step on it in order to "steal" the valuable object.

5. They will also tape five pieces of numbered (1 through 5) butcher paper (large enough to stand on) at the front of the room.

6. After recess the teacher will let the five students come back into the classroom first. The thief will steal the valuable object and hide it somewhere in the room. The other four students will simply take their seats.

7. The teacher will then let the rest of the students and the detective come back into the classroom.

8. The detective will announce that a valuable object has been stolen, and that there are five suspects.

9. The detective will call the suspects to the front of the room for a lineup.

10. The detective will instruct each suspect where to stand during the lineup (on one of the numbered pieces of butcher paper, although this needs to be done as unobtrusively as possible, so as not to give away what is happening).

11. The detective will refer to each suspect by a number, saying, "Suspect Number One, did you commit the crime?"

12. All the suspects will say no and then take their seats.

13. When the lineup is over, the detective will pick up the piece of butcher paper in front of the table and compare it with each of the five pieces of butcher paper at the front of the room. The set of footprints taken from "the scene of the crime" should match one of the sets of footprints at the lineup. The detective should be able to reveal the name of the thief.

FOOTPRINTS FOUND AT THE SCENE OF A CRIME ARE OFTEN ONE OF THE MAIN CLUES THAT HELP POLICE CATCH CRIMINALS.